THE SCH

'All right, Briggsy,' whispered Jonathan as they reached the top of the stairs. You've proved your point. Let's go back down, Hadley's getting nervous.'

'You mean you are. I'm going to explore.'

Briggs took a few cautious steps along the pitch-black corridor – then stopped with a gasp of horror.

A billowing white shape had appeared in front of him. It had arms and legs and a blobby head and it was floating towards him moaning hideously.

'Spooks!' yelled Briggsy.

Whirling round he rushed past Jonathan, thundered down the staircase, across the hall and disappeared into the night.

A Red Fox Book

Published by Random House Children's Books
20 Vauxhall Bridge Road, London SW1V 2SA

A division of Random House UK Ltd
London Melbourne Sydney Auckland
Johannesburg and agencies throughout the world

First published by Piccadilly Press Ltd 1989

Text © Terrance Dicks 1989
Illustrations © Adriano Gon 1989

Red Fox edition 1991
Reprinted 1992

Printed and bound in Great Britain by
Cox & Wyman Ltd, Reading, Berkshire

ISBN 0 09 974620 4

Terrance Dicks

JONATHAN'S GHOST
THE SCHOOL SPIRIT

Illustrated by Adriano Gon

RED FOX

CHAPTER ONE

The Haunted Bus

'Here we go, here we go, here we go!' sang the coach-load of schoolkids happily. 'Here we go, here we go, here we go-oo! Here we go, here we go, here we go! Here we go-o, here we go!'

Jonathan turned to his friend, a small bespectacled boy called Timothy. 'I'm not mad about the words – or the tune either come to that.'

Timothy, a keen musician, nodded. 'It's got a certain rhythmic force. But as a musical statement, it definitely lacks variety.'

'Here we go, here we go, here we go!'

1

carolled their schoolmates cheerfully, launching into the umpteenth chorus.

Jonathan grinned. 'Well, at least they're enjoying themselves.'

'And driving the teachers crazy at the same time,' pointed out Timothy. 'Sort of a fringe benefit.'

Jonathan nodded thoughtfully. 'Can't be bad! Shall we?'

He and Timothy raised their voices. 'Here we go, here we go, here we go . . .'

They were sitting at the back of the specially-hired mini bus on the way to a school weekend trip.

Most schools run something of the kind. A mixed group of pupils and teachers spend a weekend at some country retreat. There's a bit of study, a bit of sport and a lot of messing about. No-one's quite sure what it's supposed to achieve, but people seem to enjoy it.

Most people, that is.

Mr Fox, Jonathan's form master, was sitting in the front seat next to the art master, a fiery Welshman called Huw Hughes.

Mr Fox was red-haired, thin faced and at

the moment, a picture of gloom. 'What beats
me is the way I keep volunteering each year.
Like the victim signing on for another turn
on the rack. Why do we do it, Huw? Why *do*
we do it?'

'Well, I dunno about you, boyo. It's a combination of things with me. A chance to drink in the beauties of nature, the opportunity to watch keen young minds develop, and the beer in the village pub.'

'There is that,' agreed Mr Fox, cheering up. 'With any luck, we'll get there in time for a pint before closing time.'

'If we manage to find the place,' said Huw Hughes. 'New digs this time, remember.'

At the back of the coach, Timothy was explaining things to Jonathan who was fairly new at the school.

'I shall miss Farrow's Farm. Mrs Farrow's cooking was terrific.'

'Why the change?'

'Old Farmer Farrow retired and sold the place. The new owner said "he didn't want no blasted kids traipsing around".' Timmy said the last bit in a thick Mummerset accent.

'So where are we going then?'

'To the Old Manor House,' said Timmy impressively. 'The squire died just recently and the place went to some nephew from London. Apparently he's keen to make the Old Manor earn its keep, and when the school asked him about having us there he jumped at it.'

'Doesn't know what he's in for, does he? What's the place like?'

'Nobody knows. The old squire was pretty much a hermit, and he never let anyone inside the place. I think the Headmaster visited it when they signed the agreement. Apparently he said it was "interesting and picturesque".'

'Sounds – ouch!' yelled Jonathan.

The ouch was caused by a sharp sting on his ear. 'What's the matter?' asked Timothy. 'Insect bite?'

Jonathan picked a tightly-wadded V of paper from his lap. 'A human insect – with a good strong rubber band.'

Timothy looked at the row of seat-backs

ahead of them. 'Who, though?'

'I've a pretty good idea,' said Jonathan. 'Don't worry, he won't be able to resist having a gloat.'

Sure enough, a grinning face appeared round the back of a seat several rows ahead. A big hand appeared too, with a thick rubber band looped round one finger. 'All right, Jonno?'

It was Basher Briggs, the nearest thing they had to a school bully. He and Jonathan had tangled several times before, and somehow or other Briggs had always come off worst.

He was about to come off worst again.

Above Jonathan's head, a familiar voice said, 'Dear oh dear, some people never learn, do they?'

Jonathan looked up. Stretched out in the luggage rack above his head, using Jonathan's rucksack as a sort of pillow, was a boy of his own age. He wore baggy grey shorts held up by a cricket belt, a grey flannel shirt and grubby white tennis shoes.

It wasn't the way kids liked to dress today – but Dave wasn't exactly your everyday kid.

Dave was a ghost.

Way back in World War Two a robot-bomb, a buzz-bomb as they were known then, had hit the roof of his house, destroying Dave's attic bedroom and Dave as well.

The bomb damage had eventually been repaired and years later Jonathan's family had moved into the house. Jonathan soon discovered that Dave, or rather his ghost, was still very much around.

Once Jonathan had got over the shock, he and Dave had become good friends – best mates, as Dave put it. But Jonathan had soon discovered that having a ghost for a friend wasn't without problems.

Much of the time, Dave was around but invisible. Even when he was visible, like now, only Jonathan could see him – which meant Jonathan sometimes seemed to be talking to himself. But the real problem was that Dave insisted on being helpful – and Dave's help could be embarrassing to say the least. Jonathan had a terrible feeling Dave was going to be helpful now.

Jonathan stood up pretending to make sure his rucksack was secure. 'I'll deal with Briggsy later, Dave, don't make a fuss.'

'Don't worry, mate, discretion is our watchword.'

Dave vanished, leaving a ghostly chuckle behind.

Jonathan sat down resignedly. Something was going to happen – it was just a matter of when.

Dave's well-meaning efforts had already given Jonathan a bit of a reputation in school. Nothing specific, just a feeling that odd things seemed to happen when he was around. Jonathan hated it, and was desperately trying to live it down.

Now he sat staring up the aisle at where Briggs was sitting.

He almost missed it at first.

Something rose in the air from Briggsy's seat and hovered above it. It was a sort of circle, a loop . . .

It was a thick rubber band.

Hooked into the band was a piece of paper, folded many times into a sort of stubby V – one of Briggsy's missiles.

Rubber band and missile floated down the centre aisle of the bus – and hovered just behind the two teachers.

The band stretched into an oval, pulled back by the V – and the paper V shot forwards hitting Huw Hughes on the back of his neck.

He leaped to his feet and turned round with a roar of rage – just as Briggsy yelled and jumped up too, staring at the rubber band that was suddenly looped round his hand . . .

CHAPTER TWO
Dracula's Castle

Huw Hughes shot down the aisle, hauled Briggsy halfway out of his seat and shook him till his teeth rattled. 'Now just you listen to me, boyo! I know we relax the rules a bit on the school trip – but that does not entitle you to assault a teacher with a deadly weapon, understand?'

Briggs nodded dumbly. Dropping him back in his seat the still-seething teacher returned to the front of the bus.

'Wonder what got into old Briggsy?' said Timothy curiously.

Jonathan grinned. 'Got a bit over-confident, didn't he?'

Timmy looked thoughtfully at him. 'You know, Jonathan, it's a funny thing . . . '

Jonathan knew exactly what Timothy was going to say. Whenever anyone hassled Jonathan, somehow things always turned out badly for that person. It was just the sort of thinking he wanted to discourage.

To his relief there was a timely interruption. Mr Fox, who had been deep in conversation with the driver, turned round and shouted. 'Quiet a minute, you lot!'

'Foxy's going to make a speech,' said Jonathan.

Someone heard the last word and took it up. 'Speech, speech!' they shouted.

Mr Fox glared at his mutinous audience until they fell silent. 'We are now very close to the Old Manor House,' he began.

The announcement was greeted with cheers.

'However, since this is our first visit, no-one is sure exactly how to get there.'

There were boos and cries of 'Shame!' and 'Who organised this disaster anyway?'

Someone who'd been studying Politics shouted, 'Resign! Resign!'

Like the Prime Minister at Question Time, Foxy pressed on. 'We are therefore going to stop at the village pub, which we do know how to find . . . '

Shouts of 'I bet!' and more ironic cheers.

' . . . in order to get precise directions for the last stage of the journey,' Foxy concluded. 'Younger boys will remain outside. Hadley and Sutton and other sixth formers will collect refreshment orders and money from their fellows.'

Foxy sat down amidst more cheers and soon they were drawing up outside the little village pub which sat, like a Tourist Board poster, on the village green.

There were wooden benches and tables outside, and everyone jostled for a place while the sixth formers took endless orders for lemonade, coke and crisps.

Meanwhile, Foxy and Huw Hughes disappeared inside the bar to ask directions from the landlord and, everyone said knowingly, to sink a swift pint as well.

Jonathan and Timothy didn't bother with the wooden benches, and sat down on the grass by the front door, well-placed to grab two cokes when Hadley staggered past with a laden tray.

They were also well-placed to overhear the conversation when Huw Hughes and Foxy, both wiping their lips appreciatively, appeared in the doorway with a tubby balding man in an apron.

'Left down Manor Lane, then left again up Manor Drive,' he was saying. "Tis powerful overgrown, you'll just about get that coach up, I reckon.' He paused. 'Excuse me, sir,

you're sure it's the *Old* Manor you want?'

'Pretty sure,' said Foxy. He fished a folded letter out of his pocket and showed it to the landlord. 'There you are,' "The Old Manor House, Hobs Hollow." That's it, isn't it?'

The landlord peered at the letter. 'That's it, right enough. Only . . . the old squire never had anyone in the house, save that housekeeper of his. He wouldn't even have village folk there, let alone . . . '

'Let alone a parcel of juvenile hooligans from London?' said Huw Hughes cheerfully.

The landlord looked sheepish. 'Well now, sir . . . '

'The old squire's dead now though,' said Mr Fox briskly. 'The place has passed to his nephew, and he's very keen to have us – as you can see from his letter.'

The landlord shook his head. 'The old squire wouldn't have liked it when he was alive. Old Manor's got a bad reputation in these parts. It's unlucky for children. You could have chosen a better place to bring your boys, sir, and that's the truth. You'd do better to go back home.'

Still shaking his head, the landlord

disappeared into his pub. Foxy and Huw Hughes exchanged astonished glances, then Foxy raised his voice. 'Back in the coach, everyone!'

As Jonathan stood up, he was about to follow the others when he felt a tap on his shoulder. He turned and saw Dave standing in the doorway.

'That was good advice, mate. I'd get your teachers to take it if I were you.'

'What do you mean?'

'I've been getting bad feelings about this

Old Manor place – and they're getting stronger as we get nearer.'

'Bad vibrations on the spiritual plane?'

'You can take the mickey if you like, mate, but just be warned.'

And with that Dave vanished.

Jonathan went uneasily back to the coach. He'd learned quite a bit about the unseen world since meeting Dave. Not all Earthbound spirits were as harmless as his ghostly friend . . .

Soon they were on their way again, the coach jolting along ever-narrowing country lanes.

'You know what that business in the pub reminded me of ?' said Timothy.

Jonathan shook his head. 'No, what?'

'Those old Hammer horror movies they show on telly! They always start with some innocent young bloke turning up at the village inn and asking the way to Castle Dracula. And all the local peasants go "Aaargh! Don't 'ee go to Castle Dracula, young master!" And of course he never listens. Off he goes, and sooner or later – pow!'

'Well, what about it?'

'We're not listening either, are we?' Suddenly Timothy looked serious.

The coach lurched as they made a sharp right turn, and crawled up a lane so narrow that branches tapped the windows on either side.

'Heaven help us if we meet something going the other way,' said Timothy.

Jonathan said, 'Well, I wouldn't worry about it – it doesn't look as if anything's been along this lane for years and years.'

Suddenly the coach jolted to a stop. The driver, Mr Fox and Huw Hughes all got out, and everybody else poured out after them.

The coach was parked outside a set of massive iron gates. On the other side of the gates was a long gravel drive, and at the end of the drive was a sinister old building, towers and turrets rising black against the rapidly darkening sky.

'Looks as if you were right, Timothy,' whispered Jonathan. 'Dracula's Castle!'

Timothy looked horrified. 'We're not going in there, are we?'

'I doubt it. Look at those gates.'

The gates were held closed by a length of iron chain, ending in a huge rusty padlock.

Huw Hughes and Mr Fox stood staring at the gates in bafflement. There was no-one to be seen, and the house stood dark and silent.

Huw Hughes turned to the driver. 'Give 'em a toot, boyo!'

The driver honked his horn and the sound echoed all around them, shattering the evening hush.

But no-one came out to meet them. As Timothy went forward to look at the gate, Jonathan felt bony fingers gripping his arm.

He turned and saw that it was Dave, pulling him to one side.

'Listen mate,' hissed Dave fiercely. 'This is your chance.'

'Chance to what?'

'To get everyone out of here! Just you try and persuade those teachers of yours there's been some mix-up and you might as well all go home.'

'That's probably what'll happen anyway,' said Jonathan. 'Why are you so het up about it?'

'Because there's something evil, in that

21

house. Evil and angry – and hungry. It's been starved up till now because the place has been more or less empty. But if you lot turn up . . .'

'But the place is empty,' protested Jonathan. 'No-one seems to live there.'

'I wasn't talking about anyone alive,' said Dave, and disappeared.

CHAPTER THREE

Sinister Welcome

The two teachers stood staring at the locked gates.

'I just don't understand it,' said Mr Fox. 'The Head made the arrangements ages ago, and he got a letter of confirmation back from the new owner. Look, here it is.'

He produced the letter, the same one he'd shown the landlord of the pub.

'No use waving letters at me, boyo,' said Huw Hughes sourly. 'Letters won't get us through that gate. I reckon we might as well pack up and go home.'

Mr Fox clawed at his hair. 'All the way back to London? We'd arrive in the middle of the night. How would we get all the boys back to their homes?'

'I'm pretty sure I could climb over that gate, sir,' said Hadley.

He sounded, thought Jonathan, like one of those young officers in old war movies – the brave but dim ones who volunteer for suicide missions. Still, thought Jonathan, Hadley was Captain of Games, and Head Boy as well so no doubt he had a position to keep up.

Mr Fox had no use for heroics either. 'I really don't see how that would improve the situation, Hadley. You'd be inside, we'd still be outside and the gate would still be locked.'

'I could go up to the house and see if there's anyone there, sir.'

'He's like the mug in horror movies,' whispered Timothy. 'There's always someone at the beginning who says, "Vampires? Superstitious nonsense. *I'll* walk home through the old dark churchyard . . . " And you know straight away what's going to happen to *him*.'

'If there was anyone in the house, Hadley,' Mr Fox was saying, 'they would presumably have come to the gate and let us in.'

'Then Mr Hughes is right, sir, we might as well pack up and go home.'

Mr Fox looked wildly from Hadley to Huw Hughes, feeling trapped. Somehow going or staying were both equally unappealing.

His dilemma was resolved by the sound of an ancient sports car which puttered up the lane behind them.

A tall, balding, bespectacled man leaped out, waving a bunch of keys. 'I say, I'm frightfully sorry.'

'Ah, Mr Davenport,' said Mr Fox frostily. 'There you are.'

'I had to go into town to pick up more supplies and the old bus broke down three times on the way back.'

Jonathan nudged Timothy. 'I'm not surprised, it looks as if it belongs in a motor museum.'

Mr Davenport's car was a huge green Bentley with big leather straps round the body – presumably to hold it together, thought Jonathan.

Mr Davenport was wrestling with the padlock and chains. 'Give us a hand somebody, will you?'

Hadley, keen as ever, ran to help. The rusty gates creaked open, and soon the coach was trundling up the gravel drive.

Another of Mr Davenport's keys unlocked the creaky front door, and he went inside. They saw the flare of a match, and soon a dim yellowish light revealed a huge oak-panelled hall.

'Gas lighting,' explained Mr Davenport proudly. 'Quite a curiosity really.'

Clutching their luggage the little party shuffled none too eagerly inside.

Mr Davenport turned to the two teachers. 'If you'd like to come with me, gentlemen, we'll see about getting organised.'

'Right, you lot,' said Mr Fox. 'Just wait here quietly till we get back. Hadley, you're in charge.'

The three adults disappeared further into the house, leaving an uneasy group of boys behind them. Jonathan couldn't help noticing that Briggsy, usually the biggest loud-mouth in the class, was the quietest and most uneasy-looking of them all.

Creeping up behind him, Jonathan said, 'Boo!' right in his ear.

Briggsy went white and jumped a foot in the air. 'Pack it up, Jonno, you could give someone a heart-attack.'

'All right, Dent, no clowning,' said Hadley nervously.

'Sorry,' said Jonathan. He turned to Timothy. 'It does look a bit sinister, doesn't it?'

Timmy gulped, trying to put a brave face on it. 'Oh, I don't know. Just your average everyday haunted house.'

They were standing at the foot of a huge staircase, which led upwards into pitch darkness. There was even the traditional suit of armour standing at its foot. Family portraits lined the oak-panelled walls of the hall. Between them were shields, crossed swords, and various antique weapons.

Two huge portraits hung to one side of the big staircase. One showed a thin, white-faced man in the dress of an eighteenth-century clergyman. He was holding a hymn-book and wearing a determinedly pious expression.

The other portrait showed a tough but cheerful-looking character in eighteenth-century riding dress. He carried a sporting gun and a brandy-flask, and there were gun-dogs at his feet.

For all their outward differences the two men were strangely alike, and somehow Jonathan felt sure they must be brothers.

For some reason, he found the two portraits strangely compelling. He was gazing at them in fascination when raised voices made him

aware that an argument had broken out.

Briggsy had recovered his nerve and was being his old obnoxious self. He was picking on Timothy.

'Haunted house!' he jeered. 'Ghosts! Trust a weed like you to believe in that rubbish!' He saw Jonathan watching him and broadened his attack. 'I suppose you believe in spooks as well.'

'I like to keep an open mind,' said Jonathan. 'Of course, to do that you have to have one to keep open.'

Briggsy clenched his fists. Then he unclenched them. He wasn't very bright, but he was bright enough to remember that all his previous attempts to thump Jonathan had ended in disaster.

'Well, I'm not scared,' he boasted. 'I'm going to take a look upstairs. Coming, Jonno – or are you too scared?'

Jonathan sighed. 'All right, if you insist.'

'Now just a minute,' said Hadley.

'Don't get your knickers in a twist, Hadders,' said Briggs. 'We'll just go to the top of the stairs.'

He set off up the big staircase, and Jonathan followed.

He remembered all Dave's warnings – but it was too late to think about that.

The first part of the journey was all right, they were still in the circle of light from the hall. But the top of the staircase was in deep shadow, and the passageway beyond in almost total darkness.

Hadley's voice came floating upwards. 'You

chaps all right? You'd better come down now.'

'All right, Briggsy,' whispered Jonathan as they reached the top of the stairs. 'You've proved your point. Let's go back down, Hadley's getting nervous.'

'You mean you are. I'm going to explore.'

Briggs took a few cautious steps along the pitch-black corridor – then stopped with a gasp of horror.

A billowing white shape had appeared in front of him. It had arms and legs and a blobby head and it was floating towards him moaning hideously.

'Spooks!' yelled Briggsy.

Whirling round he rushed past Jonathan, thundered down the staircase, across the hall and disappeared into the night.

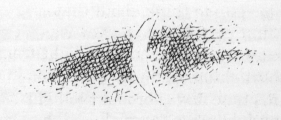

CHAPTER FOUR
Ghost Story

'As a matter of fact, the Old Manor *is* supposed to be haunted,' said Mr Davenport over supper. 'It all goes back to our family scandal – The Dark Deed of the Davenports. Now I've inherited I'm planning to write a book about it. I'm a historian, you know. While uncle was alive he always refused to give me access to the family papers – the library here is full of them. The whole story is very extensively documented, but it's been a family tradition to hush everything up. I think it's time it was brought to light.'

Despite his late arrival and his vague, scholarly manner, Mr Davenport seemed to have things surprisingly well organised. The cupboards in the enormous stone-flagged kitchen had been well stocked with food, and there was an old gas fridge and an even older cooking range, both still in working order.

The ever-efficient Hadley had soon organised a jobs rota and now they were tucking into sausages and chips washed down by mugs of steaming cocoa.

All this was after the panic caused by Briggsy's ghost-sighting had died down.

There had been utter pandemonium at the time.

Some of the more timid souls had joined Briggsy in a stampede from the house, while the rest had just milled about in confusion.

The intrepid Hadley had dashed up the stairs to save Jonathan from the spooks and found him standing quietly at the top of the stairs, looking thoughtfully along the corridor.

'What's happening?' Hadley had gasped. 'Where's the ghost?'

Jonathan had his own ideas about that, but all he'd said at the time was, 'I think it was just a flapping curtain on that window down there. Briggsy got himself all worked up and panicked when he saw something move.'

They'd gone back down the stairs, re-assured the others, and recaptured the fleeing Briggsy who was dashing down the lane apparently with the intention of running all the way back to London.

Poor old Briggs had had his leg pulled rotten after that, though not by Jonathan, and eventually the fuss had all died down.

Nevertheless, Jonathan was keenly interested in Mr Davenport's story. 'What is this Dark Deed of the Davenports, then?'

In a nice well-lit kitchen with hot food inside them, everyone was ready for a good ghost story and they all settled down to listen.

'Did anyone notice those two portraits in the hall?' Mr Davenport began.

'I did,' said Jonathan. 'Some sort of parson and a jolly-looking squire. They looked as if they might be brothers.'

'So they were,' said Mr Davenport. 'Back in the eighteenth century. The younger brother, the parson, was what you might call a high-flyer. Brilliant scholar, renowned for piety

and good works, everyone reckoned he'd finish up as a bishop. But he didn't quite make it for some reason, and eventually he came home and became parish priest of the local church.' Mr Davenport took a swig of cocoa. 'By this time his father had died and the elder brother was installed as the local squire. Now the elder brother was a very different type. Mad about hunting, shooting and fishing, rode to hounds every day in the season. Fond of the bottle, and even fonder of a tumble with the local girls.'

Briggs, now his old self again, said, 'Wor-hor-hey!'

'Briggs!' Mr Fox said sharply.

Mr Davenport coughed, and gave an embarrassed look at the two teachers.

'Sounds like a man after my own heart,' said Huw Hughes cheerfully.

Mr Fox said drily, 'I take it the two brothers did not get on well together?'

'They most certainly didn't! In fact, their quarrels were very soon the talk of the countryside. The priest was always reproving his brother about his wicked life, and the squire was always telling him to – well, get lost, I suppose.'

Mr Davenport paused dramatically. 'It all came to a head one dark and stormy night. The story goes that there was a particularly wild party going on at the hall. Unfortunately, the priest chose that night to visit his brother. He entered to find a scene of terrible debauchery.'

Briggsy started to say, 'Wor-hor- ' again.

'Shut up, Briggs, or I'll send you for a cold shower,' said Mr Fox. 'Forgive him, Mr Davenport, it's the hormones you know. Any hint of a mention of the opposite, er, gender, and he becomes positively rabid. Do go on.'

'Well, apparently the brothers had one last

terrible quarrel – which ended when the squire produced a pistol and shot his brother dead.'

The audience gave a satisfying gasp, and Mr Davenport went on, 'All the guests fled in horror, and the squire himself disappeared abroad soon afterwards.'

Timothy was goggle-eyed. 'What happened next?'

'The family tried to hush it all up. They said the priest died in a shooting accident and buried him with suspicious speed in the family chapel. But of course the story soon got about. The countryside was filled with rumours for years.'

'What happened to the squire?' asked Jonathan.

'He eventually came back to England and was promptly killed – in a duel probably. He's supposed to be buried in the grounds – in an unmarked grave.'

'Who haunts the Manor then?' asked Jonathan. 'The murdered priest or the wicked squire?'

'Well, both brothers have been sighted over the years. Mind, I've been living here for a couple of months now and I haven't seen any sign of them,' said Mr Davenport. 'And apparently there's the ghost of a little girl as well. So there you are then, you can't say we don't give good value. Not just one ghost, but three!'

'Do they just appear and disappear?' asked Timothy, 'or are they supposed to be dangerous?'

Mr Davenport looked uneasy. 'Well, there have been a few – accidents – over the years, mostly to children who climbed into the grounds to play. One was nearly killed. No local child has been near this place for years. So, be careful tomorrow when you're out and about.'

Mr Fox rose. 'And on that cheerful note we shall all go to bed – after the washing-up, of course. Your bedrooms are on the first and second floors – Mr Davenport will show you where they are. Breakfast will be at eight o'clock sharp. Be sure to consult with Hadley to see if you are on breakfast duty.'

Mr Fox paused. 'The gas lighting only covers the ground floor, so Hadley and the older boys will all be given candle-holders and candles. They will be responsible for seeing you don't make a bonfire of yourselves.'

When the washing-up was done, they all filed upstairs to bed.

Most of them were sleeping in one huge room converted into a dormitory. But there weren't quite enough beds in it, so a couple of boys were going to have to sleep in rooms by themselves. They drew lots and Jonathan and Timothy lost out. Timothy was nervous, but Jonathan was quite pleased.

Each was given his own candle, and off they went to their separate rooms.

Not long afterwards, Jonathan was lying in bed, which happened to be an enormous four-poster. He'd pulled back the bed-curtains – with them drawn it was like sleeping in a musty velvet tent.

He'd pulled back the window curtain too. Through the open window he could see the crescent moon against a background of black, wind-driven storm clouds.

On the little night-stand beside his bed, his stub of candle was burning low.

Suddenly it guttered and went out.

Jonathan didn't move. He just lay there, waiting.

Soon his window curtain began to move.

A billowing white shape appeared.

It had a blobby head and stubby arms and legs.

It moved towards him making weird noises. 'Woo-oo-oo,' it moaned. 'Woo-oo-oo!'

Jonathan yawned. 'Come off it, Dave. I've seen your spook act before. It wasn't all that convincing the first time!'

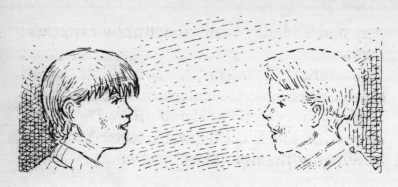

CHAPTER FIVE

The Buried Past

Dave threw aside the sheet and perched on the end of the bed, grinning cheekily. 'It was good enough for old Briggsy, wasn't it?'

'Briggsy's a moron,' said Jonathan impatiently. 'Look, Dave, what do you think you're up to, carrying on like this. I thought you promised not to make life difficult for me any more.'

Dave's grin faded. 'Believe me, mate, I am not just mucking about. I'm trying to save you from some horrible fate. I thought if I gave Briggsy a good scare you might all change your minds and go home after all.'

'But why are you so keen for us to go? Is

this place really haunted – apart from you, I mean?'

'Haunted? I'll say it's haunted! I reckon there are at least three Earthbound spirits.'

'Mr Davenport said there were three ghosts,' said Jonathan. He gave Dave a potted version of the story Davenport had told them over supper.

Dave listened thoughtfully. 'Well, that could account for it, I suppose.'

'Have you managed to communicate at all?'

Dave shook his head. 'Not really, we're not on the same wavelength you might say. You see, Earthbound spirits are all wrapped up in whatever it is that's keeping them Earthbound. I'm different. I come back to Earth because I want to, with them, it's usually something pretty fierce, sort of obsessing them. Hatred, revenge . . . or maybe a need for justice, wanting the truth to come out . . . Like that Spitfire Pilot we ran into at your Great-Aunt's house.'

'So what is it with this lot?'

'It's all mixed up,' said Dave. 'One of them, the worst, is more or less pure evil. All I pick up off him is like a rage to hurt or destroy – as if he wanted revenge on the whole human race. The other one's just angry and baffled, as if there's something he wants to do and can't . . . '

'And the third spirit?'

'I think that must be the little girl. It just feels sort of sad and lost . . . '

Jonathan sat up in bed, thinking hard. The trouble with this sort of problem was, there was no-one you could share it with. He certainly couldn't go to Foxy or Huw Hughes.

'Dave, do you *really* think we're in danger? Could one of these spirits actually hurt someone? I mean, what could they do – materialise and give someone a nasty fright, I suppose, but what else?'

'You just don't understand,' said Dave despairingly. 'There's so much bottled-up psychic energy in this place it's like a volcano. Someone could be driven mad, or even killed. They could lose their soul.'

'Can't you get in touch with them, find out what they want? Maybe we could help, like we did with the Spitfire Pilot.'

'I can try,' said Dave dubiously. 'But it's dangerous for me as well, you know.'

'Why, what could they do to you? I mean, you're a . . . ' Jonathan broke off, not sure how to put what he wanted to say.

'A ghost already?' said Dave. 'Maybe I am, but that doesn't mean I've got nothing to lose. If I start messing about with spirits as powerful as these, I could get wiped out on the spiritual plane.'

'What does that mean?'

'It could mean I didn't exist at all – in your world or in the next.'

Jonathan looked helplessly at him. 'So what do we do?'

'Lay low – and whatever you do, don't go out of your room till daylight. I'll sort of watch over things as best I can.'

'Is there anything I can do to help?'

'I'm afraid not,' said Dave grimly. 'This is down to me. A ghost's gotta do what a ghost's gotta do . . . Wish me luck!'

And with that he faded away.

Jonathan lay back on his pillows, wondering if he would ever get to sleep. The affairs of the spirit world seemed confused and complicated, he thought. He'd got used to Dave, but it was strange to think that there

were ghosts even Dave was frightened of . . .
The pillows were soft and the room was dark
and Jonathan had had a tiring day. Despite
all his worries he found himself drifting off to
sleep.

The trouble with going to sleep is that
you're liable to dream . . .

*Jonathan was drifting slowly on a sea of
darkness. It was a sensation he'd felt before,
and somehow he knew that he wasn't just
asleep, he was out of his body, drifting on
what Dave would have called the spiritual
plane.*

*There was a girl, somewhere ahead of him
in the distance. She was young and thin and
frightened-looking, wearing an old-fashioned
nightgown. She was calling him, she wanted
him to go with her . . . But Jonathan still had
Dave's warnings in his head and he wasn't
sure . . .*

*All at once there was a man with the girl – a
tough-looking man in riding dress with a
smoking pistol in his hand. It was the squire,
the one who'd murdered his brother . . .*

He wanted Jonathan to go with him as well.

There was something he had to show him, something vitally important.

Jonathan struggled to resist. The man was a murderer, he couldn't be trusted . . .

Suddenly there was a black-clad white-faced figure in the way. It was the murdered priest. He seemed to be sending off waves of cold anger, telling Jonathan the other spirits were evil, that he mustn't listen to them . . .

Still the squire and the girl beckoned to him, the squire waving his smoking pistol.

It was strange how real it all seemed, thought Jonathan. Even though he knew it was only a dream he could actually *smell* the smoke from the squire's pistol.

Suddenly Jonathan realised he was awake.

He was awake – but he could still smell smoke.

Without even thinking about Dave's warning, Jonathan leaped out of bed and dashed out of his room.

There was a haze of smoke in the corridor outside and a nearby flickering of flames.

Smoke and light were both coming from the next room – Timothy's room.

Jonathan ran to the doorway.

Timothy lay on his bed, asleep as if in a trance.

The curtains near his bed were all ablaze.

Jonathan started to go to him – and suddenly the white-faced priest was in the doorway, barring his way.

Whatever warning the spirit was trying to give, Jonathan didn't have time for it.

He dashed straight *through* the apparition, and knocked Timothy from the bed, falling to the floor on top of him.

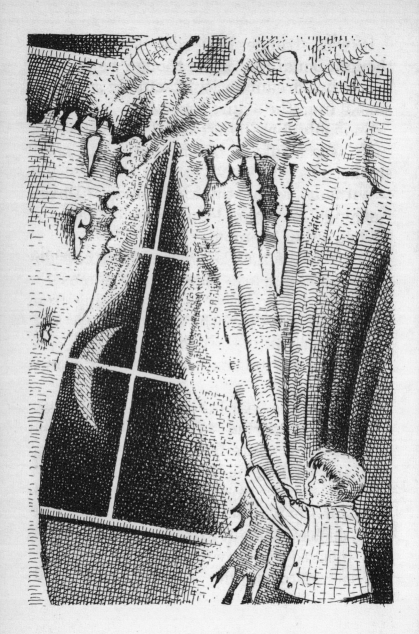

Timothy came awake with a yell of alarm, clutching wildly at him.

'Wake up, Timmy, there's a fire,' shouted Jonathan. 'Go and give the alarm.'

Timothy ran into the corridor shouting, 'Fire! Fire! Fire!'

Jonathan dragged down the blazing curtains and tried to smother them with the blankets from the bed.

Suddenly the room was full of people helping him, and soon the flames were beaten down.

Hadley came rushing in with a bucket of water which he hurled across the bed, not realising that Huw Hughes was stamping out flames on the other side.

Unfortunately, Huw Hughes stood up just as Hadley let fly with the contents of the bucket . . .

For a moment Huw Hughes just stood there, dripping quietly into the charred carpet. Then he said quietly, 'Thank you Hadley, most refreshing.'

Hadley gulped and hurried away.

Gradually everyone calmed down and Jonathan told Mr Fox what had happened.

He decided it was best to keep it simple, so he just said he'd been woken by the smell of smoke and got up to find Timmy's curtains on fire. 'I woke Timothy up and sent him to give the alarm, and did my best to smother the flames.'

'You did very well,' said Mr Fox. 'Very well indeed.' He sighed wearily. 'Well, I suppose if boys have to be given candles at least one of them is bound to be careless – and one is all it takes.' He looked down at Timothy. 'I must say I'm surprised it was you though, I thought you were such a sensible boy.'

Timothy was white-faced and shaken. 'But it wasn't, sir, I mean I didn't. I put the candle out very carefully before I went to sleep. I remember doing it.'

Timothy was very distressed and Mr Fox patted him awkwardly on the back. 'I'm sure you think you did.' He looked round the smoke-blackened room. 'However, the evidence does seem to suggest you were mistaken! Come on, we must find you somewhere else to sleep. I trust the school insurance will pay for the damage.'

Still protesting, Timmy was led away and

everyone started drifting back to their own beds.

When he got back to his room, Jonathan wasn't surprised to find Dave waiting for him.

'See?' said Dave simply. 'What did I tell you?'

Wearily Jonathan climbed back into bed. 'I suppose it could have been an accident . . .'

'Don't you believe it. There was something very sinister going on tonight. I tried to warn you, but there was no way I could overcome the evil force. It was just too powerful for me.'

'It's certainly not like Timmy to be careless,' said Jonathan thoughtfully. 'He's one of life's worriers, checks everything ten times over. You think it was one of the Earthbound spirits set fire to the curtains. Would they be able to?'

Dave nodded. 'Dead easy! It doesn't take much psychic energy to light a candle, I could do it myself. Not that I would, of course. I tell you, mate, that was no accident. One of those spirits is a killer – and it wants fresh blood!'

Jonathan had been thinking hard about what had happened – and he'd come up with a very worrying theory. 'Old Davenport was saying something about accidents,' he said. 'Accidents to kids playing in the grounds. He said no local child has been near this place for years. Do you reckon this evil spirit of yours hates children – children particularly, I mean, more than anyone else?'

Dave shrugged. 'Could do, I suppose . . . What are you getting at?'

Jonathan went on with his theory. 'Let's say I'm right, and for some reason this particular ghost hates kids. Well, there haven't been any children living here for years, and according to you, it can't go out and hunt for them . . .'

Dave nodded. 'The thing about Earthbound spirits is, they're usually tied pretty strictly to one place. They can't go wandering round the country the way I do.'

'It'd just have to lie in wait then, wouldn't it?' said Jonathan slowly. 'Maybe pounce on some village kid who was daft enough to climb into the grounds. And when they stopped coming, it'd just get hungrier and hungrier . . . And then we turn up. A whole busload of lambs, wandering into the lion's den. Victims all over the place . . . it can pick and choose!'

'That's right, mate – and you know who it's liable to pick next, don't you? You!'

'Me?' said Jonathan uneasily. 'Why me?'

'Spoiled its fun, didn't you? It was all set to turn young Timmy to a crisp and you interfered. It's not going to like that . . . '

Jonathan drew a deep breath. 'So what do I do?'

'Stay awake,' said Dave simply. 'As much as you can, anyway. I'll do my best to look after you, but this thing's a lot more powerful than I am . . . You stay here, and I'll scout around, see if it's still hanging about. And, remember, don't go to sleep!'

Before Jonathan could say anything, Dave just faded away.

Jonathan piled his pillows up high, re-lit his candle, and dug out a biology textbook from his knapsack. 'A good dose of scientific fact,' he thought, 'that's what I need.'

He did his best to stay awake.

But when you're young and you've had a tiring and exciting day, staying awake is one of the hardest things to do.

Even if going to sleep could cost you your life.

The candle flame waved and flickered and the words of the textbook blurred before his eyes . . .

Jonathan thought about getting up, walking round the room. But even as he was thinking about it, his head nodded and he was dreaming . . .

He dreamed he was floating away on a warm dark sea . . .

He didn't see the dark figure that materialised in the corner of the room, eyes gleaming with hate.

It raised its hand. The heavy old-fashioned bedspread rose in the air, hovered, and wrapped itself round Jonathan's head and shoulders. Still drifting in a warm soft darkness, Jonathan suddenly became aware that the dark sea had become solid. It was suffocating him, choking him. The worst thing about it was that he couldn't move . . .

He fought for breath, a roaring in his head. He felt himself sinking . . .

A sudden sharp pain in his ankle jolted him awake.

Jonathan panicked, wrestling with the bedspread, struggling to get free. He realised that someone was helping, pulling the bedspread from his face . . .

Panting, Jonathan struggled clear, and immediately the bedspread dropped to the ground, just a harmless piece of cloth.

Dave was looking at him in concern. 'You all right, mate?'

'I think so . . . What happened?'

'It tricked me,' said Dave bitterly. 'Sort of lured me away. Finally I realised, shot back here – and found the bedspread attacking you like a boa-constrictor.'

'Why's my ankle so sore?'

'Well, you were just lying there. I had to give you a kick on the ankle to wake you up!'

'Thanks a lot!' said Jonathan. Then he looked serious. 'I mean it, Dave, thanks. You saved my life.'

Dave looked embarrassed. 'Shouldn't have left you, should I?'

'What do we do now?'

'Sit it out till morning. I'll see you don't nod off. Don't worry, I'm a ghost, I don't need sleep.'

Dave and Jonathan sat chatting through the hours of darkness, and every time Jonathan's head nodded, Dave's bony elbow jolted him awake.

Finally Dave looked out of the window. A few pale streaks were appearing in the sky and the birds were starting to kick up a racket. 'It's nearly dawn now. Even the worst evil spirit's powers aren't so strong when the day's beginning. I reckon you can risk a few hours' kip . . .'

CHAPTER SIX
Ghostly Attack

It took a long time for Jonathan to get off to sleep, even though he was aware of Dave sitting on the end of the bed watching over him.

He didn't really drop off until well after dawn, and even then his sleep was fitful and uneasy.

He was awakened by someone shaking him. 'Jonathan! Wake up! Wake up!'

He opened his eyes to find Timmy standing over him. 'Come on Jonathan, wake up, we've overslept. We'll be late for breakfast.'

Jonathan staggered out of bed and after a quick wash and dress he and Timothy hurried downstairs.

As they crossed the hall, Timothy came to a sudden halt before the two big portraits. 'That picture, it was in my dream. I dreamed he was there in my room. He was holding a candle high above his head.'

'Who the wicked squire?'

'No, no, the other one – the murdered priest. Now, why should I dream that?'

Jonathan tried to reassure him. 'Why shouldn't you? You saw the portrait last night, then Mr Davenport told us the story. I expect it all got mixed up in your mind. Dreams are often like that, mix-ups of what's been going on. Some people think dreams are just the mind clearing its memory banks.'

Timothy said seriously, 'I didn't leave that candle burning last night, you know. I really didn't. You know what a fuss-pot I am. I was terrified of starting a fire the minute I got the candle and I checked it was really out at least a dozen times.'

'I believe you, Timmy,' said Jonathan gently. 'I really do.'

'Then how did the fire start?'

'Beats me,' said Jonathan. But his mind was filled with the picture of Timothy and the blazing curtains.

Those curtains had been burning from the top. There was no way a knocked-over candle could have come anywhere near the place where the fire had begun . . .

The fire had been started deliberately. But who would have done it? Surely the obvious candidate was the wicked squire. But why had Timothy dreamed about the priest?

Maybe the priest had tried to stop it, just as he'd warned Jonathan away from the fire last night. Timothy had seen him and got muddled . . .

Jonathan sighed. 'Never mind, Timmy, just try and forget about it. Let's go in for some breakfast.'

First thing on the agenda after breakfast was Applied Botany. This boiled down to a wander round the Old Manor House's incredibly large and overgrown garden, looking vaguely for any interesting plants.

'There's a pond and a little stream right down the bottom of the garden,' said Mr Davenport. 'Watch out for the pond though, it's surprisingly deep. In fact the locals say it's bottomless.'

It was a hot sunny morning and they were all bursting to get outside. Before long everyone was happily pottering along the banks of the stream or studying the edge of the pond, which was rich in plant life.

Foxy and Huw Hughes supervised from beneath the shade of a convenient oak tree.

There was frogspawn in the pond and Robbie Peters, one of the younger boys, had come armed with a jam-jar and a fishing net. Jonathan watched as he leaned over the pond, reaching out for a big clump of frogspawn.

He saw Hadley come up behind Peters, and assumed he was going to offer to help, making use of his longer reach.

Then he saw the expression on Hadley's face. It was cold and cruel. In fact it didn't look like Hadley at all.

Hadley looked like someone else – someone different and yet familiar. To Jonathan's astonishment, this strange Hadley leaned forwards and deliberately shoved Peters into the pond.

Jonathan reacted without thinking.

He dived in, grabbed the frantically struggling Peters and shoved him towards the bank, where willing hands heaved them both out, dripping with weed.

Mr Fox and Huw Hughes came hurrying up.

Mr Fox looked at Jonathan. 'Well done! We'll have to put you in for the Lifesaving Medal. Now, you'd both better get back to the house and get into something dry.'

On the way Jonathan squelched over to Hadley. Somehow he just had to convince him he wasn't to blame. Hadley was staring fixedly into the pond. 'You mustn't blame yourself, Hadley, you did your best.'

Hadley stared wildly at him. 'My best – but I . . .'

'Peters slipped, and you tried to grab him but missed,' said Jonathan firmly. 'Isn't that right, Robbie?'

Little Peters couldn't really remember what had happened and he certainly wasn't going to argue with his heroic rescuer. 'Yes, that's right. I felt you trying to grab me as I slipped.'

Hadley's face cleared. 'Yes, that's right. I'd better keep the others away from the edge of the pond.'

Hadley hurried off, and Peters and Jonathan made their way back to the house for some dry clothes.

Jonathan had just finished changing in his room when Dave appeared. 'Something's happened, I can feel it.'

Jonathan told him about Hadley's strange behaviour.

'He was taken over,' said Dave at once. 'Possessed!'

'Yes, but why? What does this spirit want?'

'Death,' said Dave slowly. 'I can feel it. Somehow it was cheated of a death in the past and it wants to claim one now. It won't rest until it's killed someone.'

'I think you're right. You know what keeps worrying me, Dave? Apart from having a homicidal spook on the loose, that is?'

'What?'

'The story's all wrong.'

'What story?'

'The one Davenport told us, the Davenports' Dark Deed. It doesn't fit what's been happening – and it doesn't fit what you found out about these Earthbound spirits – or what I feel about them either.'

'How do you mean?'

'Well, all that stuff about one of them being

angry and baffled. The way I felt the girl and the squire wanted to tell me something . . . It just doesn't fit.'

'Fit what?'

Jonathan struggled to explain. 'Look, the story Davenport told us is too straight-forward, too cut and dried. Bad brother murders good brother, comes to a bad end. End of story. There's no mystery, no secret, nothing to explain what's been going on or why one of the spirits turned so murderous. Unless . . . '

'Unless what?'

'Unless the story's all wrong . . . ' Jonathan shook his head. 'But it can't be, Davenport said it was all confirmed in family records and local histories.' Jonathan got up and started pacing about the room. 'So we've got to accept that the squire did kill his brother – but maybe the story gets the reasons all wrong. Maybe the killing was – justified in some way.'

'Pretty hard to justify killing your own brother, especially when he's a priest.'

'I know,' said Jonathan gloomily. 'And where does the little girl fit in? I'm just going round in circles. The funny thing is, when Timothy's curtains were on fire I saw the priest trying to *stop* me getting to him. And Timothy dreamed he saw the *priest* holding the candle.' Jonathan came to a sudden halt in the centre of the room. 'And when Hadley was shoving poor old Peters in the pond, he looked just like the priest in the portrait!' He looked excitedly at Dave. 'I can't prove it, but I'm convinced of it. Somehow or other it's the priest who's the villain of the piece, and the priest's ghost is the murderous one . . . '

Suddenly Dave leaped from the bed and shoved Jonathan clear across the room – just as the heavy glass chandelier crashed down on the spot where he'd just been standing.

Jonathan leaned gasping against the wall. 'Thanks, Dave.' He looked at the ruins of the chandelier. 'You know, something tells me we're on the right track!'

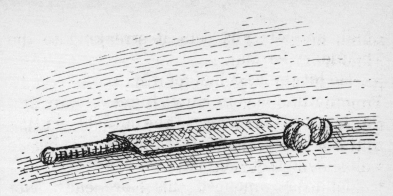

CHAPTER SEVEN

Dangerous Quest

Mr Davenport was very nice about the chandelier. He said it was an old house and bits were dropping off all the time.

As the afternoon wore on the heat became almost unbearable. Nobody really wanted to do anything but lie down in the shade and rest.

Mr Fox wasn't having that.

He organised a game of cricket. He was the captain of one side, and Huw Hughes captained the other.

Foxy won the toss, and put himself in to bat.

A nervous Timothy bowled him the first

ball, and Mr Fox sent it streaking to the boundary for four.

He hit the next ball for a six . . .

Jonathan was in Huw Hughes's team and as he stood perspiring in the outfield, waiting for his turn to bowl, Dave popped up beside him. 'Enjoying yourself ?'

Jonathan mopped his forehead. 'Not really!'

Dave gave an elaborate yawn. 'Old Foxy looks set to stay there all day. I'd offer you a bit of help, but I know you don't like me to interfere . . .'

'I think this is a special case.'

Jonathan went over to Huw Hughes who was gloomily watching the slaughter. 'Give us a chance at bowling, sir.'

'You must be mad, boy, wanting to expend energy on a day like this. Still, suit yourself.'

Next over, Huw Hughes put Jonathan on to bowl.

Jonathan faced up to the mighty Foxy.

He bowled him a slow googly.

Mr Fox smiled evilly, stepped confidently forward, and raised his bat. Somehow the ball seemed to hover for a moment. Then it

shot between his legs and took out his middle
stump.

With an outraged glare Foxy stalked from
the field.

It was Hadley's turn to face the bowling
and Jonathan sent him a sizzling fast one.

Hadley stepped confidently to meet it – but
he stumbled over some invisible obstacle and
the ball shattered his wicket.

Jonathan bowled out the next batsman too
– and the next and the next . . .

When Foxy's team were all out, Jonathan and Huw Hughes went in to open for their side.

'I warn you, I'm a terrible cricketer,' rumbled Huw Hughes.

'Just leave it all to me, sir. Keep the batting my end and we'll be okay.'

Hadley bowled the first ball, a slow twister, which seemed to check at the last minute and hover invitingly in front of Jonathan's bat.

Jonathan hit it for six.

He hit the next ball for a six and most of the rest of the over as well, varying it with the occasional four.

He was well on the way to beating Foxy's fifty when it happened. Hadley ran up to bowl his next ball. He was a fairly tricky slow bowler, but Jonathan was confident he could handle him – especially with a little help from Dave.

But suddenly Hadley wasn't a slow bowler any more. He took a long run and pounded up to the crease, his face a mask of hatred – just the way it had looked when he tried to push Peters in the pond.

The ball shot from his hand with

superhuman force – straight for Jonathan's head.

Jonathan just managed to get his bat up in time.

The force of the ball splintered the bat and the deflected ball grazed Jonathan's forehead.

For a moment the whole field of players stood frozen in astonishment.

'Are you all right?' called Foxy.

Jonathan nodded dumbly.

Hadley seemed to be dazed . . .

There was a sudden tremendous thunderclap, a flash of sheet lightning and suddenly the rain came pouring down.

'Game over,' shouted Foxy. 'We'll call it a draw, rain stopped play!'

As he ran back to the house, Jonathan wasn't thinking about cricket.

He knew he'd had another lucky escape from the power of the malignant spirit.

It seemed determined to kill somebody. And at the moment it seemed determined to kill him.

After supper Jonathan had a long talk with Mr Davenport about the family scandal. Pleased by his interest Mr Davenport took him to the study and showed him the family papers. They told the full story of the murder of the priest and the squire's flight and subsequent death.

The story was confirmed in every detail – there was even a display case with relics of the brothers, the priest's cross and hymnbook, and the squire's riding crop and brandy-flask and pistol.

When Mr Davenport was searching for a copy of the local history, Jonathan on a sudden impulse slipped the squire's gun and the priest's cross from the display case into his pocket.

Night fell as it always must, and it was time for bed.

Foxy and Huw Hughes carried out a candle patrol, checking that every candle was well and truly out.

Once they'd left Jonathan's room, Dave appeared on the end of Jonathan's bed. 'Well, now what?'

'I'm going to sleep – and if the squire turns up again, I'm going to go with him.'

'Suppose you're wrong?' said Dave. 'Suppose he is an evil spirit after all? I won't let you do it, it's far too dangerous.'

'It's too dangerous not to. You said yourself – it, whoever or whatever it is, wants a death. It's attacked three of us now – Timothy, little Peters and now me. No adults, you notice. I think my idea was right – it wants to kill a child. If I don't stop it now it's bound to get one of us eventually – most likely me, since it knows I'm on to it.'

'All right,' said Dave wearily. 'If you must, you must. I'll give you what help I can, but I can't promise too much.'

Jonathan lay back on his pillows and waited for sleep.

He fell into it almost at once, like dropping into a black pit.

Suddenly he felt he was floating.

A figure appeared before him. It was the squire, pistol in hand. He beckoned, and Jonathan followed.

All at once they were tramping through the garden, the storm howling over their heads. Not they, Jonathan realised suddenly. Somehow he wasn't with the squire any more, he was the squire, seeing events through his eyes, understanding them through his brain.

Now it was a night two hundred years ago, and he was tramping through the rain-sodden garden towards the family chapel, dreading what he would find.

He heard the sound of chanting as he drew nearer.

It seemed to be rising to a crescendo.

He reached the wooden door of the chapel and hurled it open.

A service was taking place – but no ordinary service.

It was a ceremony of evil – of devil worship. Lying on the altar was a young girl, and *standing over her was a scarlet-robed figure in a goat-mask, a knife raised high.*

As the knife swept down the squire drew the pistol from his pocket and fired – one bullet through the heart.

The robed figure fell across the body of its intended victim.

Ignoring the shrieking figures rushing past him and out into the night he strode over to the altar and snatched the mask from the high priest.

His brother's dead face stared up at him.

He lifted the fainting child from the altar and carried her back towards the house.

Suddenly Jonathan was himself again, floating once more in limbo. This time it was the girl who appeared before him, beckoning.

Once again Jonathan followed.

He knew now that she was the girl on the altar, the one the squire had saved at the cost of his brother's life.

She took him to the hall and showed him a secret panel in the wall, between the portraits of the two brothers. Inside was a sealed earthenware jar.

She raised her hand in farewell and disappeared.

Suddenly Jonathan realised he was awake – and back in his bed. He knew the truth now, knew what he must do.

With a sigh of relief Jonathan opened his eyes.

The priest was standing over him, knife in hand . . .

CHAPTER EIGHT

The Final Truth

For a moment the white face glared down at him, eyes blazing with hate.

Then the knife swept down.

Suddenly Dave appeared from nowhere, knocking aside the descending arm.

For a moment the two grappled, but the years of hate had given the priest more stored-up psychic energy than Dave could muster.

Dave was flung aside with ease and the knife arm rose again . . .

But Dave's intervention had given Jonathan the time he needed.

From under his pillow he took the silver

cross that had belonged to the priest and held it up.

For a moment the symbol of the religion he had dishonoured seemed to freeze the priest where he stood.

But only for a moment.

Slowly, the knife arm rose again.

From under the pillow Jonathan snatched the squire's pistol and trained it on the priest's heart.

The pistol was empty of course.

But in the spirit world of the ghostly priest, the pistol roared as it had two hundred years ago, and he felt the shock of the bullet in his heart.

The second, symbolic death seemed to

release him from his long years of hate-filled bondage to Earth.

The ghostly body shattered and dispersed and the knife clattered to the floor and vanished.

Jonathan fell back on his pillow with a gasp of relief and looked up at Dave. 'I think we did it,' he said. 'It's over.'

Next day, Jonathan recovered the sealed jar from the secret panel beneath the portraits. It proved to contain a thick wodge of papers sealed in a sort of oilskin parcel. Jonathan handed them over to Mr Davenport who disappeared into the study with them and wasn't seen again till dinner-time.

When supper was over Mr Davenport said, 'When you first came here I told you all the story of our family legend. I'm afraid most of it was lies. Now I'm going to tell you the story again – this time it will be the truth.'

Mr Davenport said the first part of the legend had been true enough. Failing in his ambitions, the talented young priest came home, and took up an appointment in his local church.

'Bitterly disappointed by the failure of his ambitions he sought power by other means. If he could not be God's Bishop, he would be the devil's. He became a Satanist, and recruited other local notables to his evil cult.

'His brother the squire was horrified when he heard the rumours about what was going on. At first he refused to believe it.

"Then, one night, he came to the family chapel and found an evil ceremony in progress and a child about to be sacrificed. To save the child he killed his brother, and to save the family name he fled abroad. But the dead priest had friends in high places. To save his reputation and their own, they slandered the missing squire and spread a story that turned truth on its head. When the squire returned to England to clear his name, they murdered him, and buried him on his estate in an unmarked grave.' Mr Davenport tapped the pile of papers. 'The true story and the location of the grave are both in these papers, written by the girl the squire saved from sacrifice. She was afraid to tell the truth at the time, the squire's enemies were too powerful. But luckily she left this record

behind her – and, quite by chance I
understand, Jonathan found it.'

Mr Davenport beamed round the table.
'I shall have my ancestor the squire re-buried
in the family chapel, and I shall write a book
that will clear his name!'

Everyone cheered, and then they all went
up to bed.

'What I want now is a nice night's unhaunted

...than as he climbed under the

...oked indignant. 'Well, there's a nice
...o say.'

'Oh, I don't mean you,' said Jonathan
sleepily. 'You're what you could call the
school spirit! I'm used to you . . . '

Jonathan drifted off to sleep and Dave
wandered round the house filled with
sleeping kids.

'School spirit indeed,' thought Dave. 'Well,
if I'm the school ghost, I'm entitled to do a bit
of haunting.'

He found his white sheet and floated up
and down the dark corridors.

'Woo-oo-ooo,' he wailed. 'Woo-oo-oo!'

But nobody took any notice.

They were all fast asleep.

Other great reads ❤ *from* **Red Fox**

Further Red Fox titles that you might enjoy reading are listed on the following pages. They are available in bookshops or they can be ordered directly from us.

If you would like to order books, please send this form and the money due to:

ARROW BOOKS, BOOKSERVICE BY POST, PO BOX 29, DOUGLAS, ISLE OF MAN, BRITISH ISLES. Please enclose a cheque or postal order made out to Arrow Books Ltd for the amount due, plus 30p per book for postage and packing to a maximum of £3.00, both for orders within the UK. For customers outside the UK, please allow 35p per book.

NAME _OLIVER COOPS_

ADDRESS _0208 343 9668_

Please print clearly.

Whilst every effort is made to keep prices low, it is sometimes necessary to increase cover prices at short notice. If you are ordering books by post, to save delay it is advisable to phone to confirm the correct price. The number to ring is THE SALES DEPARTMENT 071 (if outside London) 973 9700.

Other great reads from **Red Fox**

THE SNIFF STORIES   Ian Whybrow

Things just keep happening to Ben Moore. It's dead hard avoiding disaster when you've got to keep your street cred with your mates *and* cope with a family of oddballs at the same time. There's his appalling 2½ year old sister, his scatty parents who are into healthy eating and animal rights and, worse than all of these, there's Sniff! If only Ben could just get on with his scientific experiments and his attempt at a world beating *Swampbeast* score . . . but there's no chance of that while chaos is just around the corner.

ISBN 0 09 975040 6   £2.99

J.B. SUPERSLEUTH   Joan Davenport

James Bond is a small thirteen-year-old with spots and spectacles. But with a name like that, how can he help being a supersleuth?

It all started when James and 'Polly' (Paul) Perkins spotted a teacher's stolen car. After that, more and more mysteries needed solving. With the case of the Arabian prince, the Murdered Model, the Bonfire Night Murder and the Lost Umbrella, JB's reputation at Moorside Comprehensive soars.

But some of the cases aren't quite what they seem . . .

ISBN 0 09 971780 8   £2.99

Other great reads from **Red Fox**

**Discover the exciting and hilarious books of
Hazel Townson!**

THE MOVING STATUE

One windy day in the middle of his paper round, Jason Riddle
is blown against the town's war memorial statue.

But the statue moves its foot! Can this be true?

ISBN 0 09 973370 6 £1.99

ONE GREEN BOTTLE

Tim Evans has invented a fantasic new board game called
REDUNDO. But after he leaves it at his local toy shop it
disappears! Could Mr Snyder, the wily toy shop owner have
stolen the game to develop it for himself? Tim and his friend
Doggo decide to take drastic action and with the help of a
mysterious green bottle, plan a Reign of Terror.

ISBN 0 09 935490 X £2.25

THE SPECKLED PANIC

When Kip buys Venger's Speckled Truthpaste instead of
toothpaste, funny things start happening. But they get out of
control when the headmaster eats some by mistake. What terrible
truths will he tell the parents on speech day?

ISBN 0 09 956810 1 £2.25

THE CHOKING PERIL

In this sequel to *The Speckled Panic*, Herbie, Kip and Arthur
Venger the inventor attempt to reform Grumpton's litterbugs.

ISBN 0 09 950530 4 £2.25

Other great reads *from* **Red Fox**

The Maggie Series   Joan Lingard

MAGGIE 1: THE CLEARANCE

Sixteen-year-old Maggie McKinley's dreading the prospect of
a whole summer with her granny in a remote Scottish glen. But
the holiday begins to look more exciting when Maggie meets
the Frasers. She soon becomes best friends with James and
spends almost all her time with him. Which leads, indirectly,
to a terrible accident . . .

ISBN 0 09 947730 0   £1.99

MAGGIE 2: THE RESETTLING

Maggie McKinley's family has been forced to move to a high
rise flat and her mother is on the verge of a nervous breakdown.
As her family begins to rely more heavily on her, Maggie finds
less and less time for her schoolwork and her boyfriend James.
The pressures mount and Maggie slowly realizes that she alone
must control the direction of her life.

ISBN 0 09 949220 2   £1.99

MAGGIE 3: THE PILGRIMAGE

Maggie is now seventeen. Though a Glaswegian through and
through, she is very much looking forward to a cycling holiday
with her boyfriend James. But James begins to annoy Maggie
and tensions mount. Then they meet two Canadian boys and
Maggie finds she is strongly attracted to one of them.

ISBN 0 09 951190 8   £2.50

MAGGIE 4: THE REUNION

At eighteen, Maggie McKinley has been accepted for university
and is preparing to face the world. On her first trip abroad, she
flies to Canada to a summer au pair job and a reunion with Phil,
the Canadian student she met the previous summer. But as usual
in Maggie's life, events don't go quite as planned . . .

ISBN 0 09 951260 2   £2.50

Other great reads ← *from* **Red Fox**

Discover the great animal stories of Colin Dann

JUST NUFFIN

The Summer holidays loomed ahead with nothing to look forward to except one dreary week in a caravan with only Mum and Dad for company. Roger was sure he'd be bored.

But then Dad finds Nuffin: an abandoned puppy who's more a bundle of skin and bones than a dog. Roger's holiday is transformed and he and Nuffin are inseparable. But Dad is adamant that Nuffin must find a new home. Is there *any* way Roger can persuade him to change his mind?

ISBN 0 09 966900 5   £2.99

KING OF THE VAGABONDS

'You're very young,' Sammy's mother said, 'so heed my advice. Don't go into Quartermile Field.'

His mother and sister are happily domesticated but Sammy, the tabby cat, feels different. They are content with their lot, never wondering what lies beyond their immediate surroundings. But Sammy is burningly curious and his life seems full of mysteries. Who is his father? Where has he gone? And what is the mystery of Quartermile Field?

ISBN 0 09 957190 0   £2.99

Other great reads ~~ *from* **Red Fox**

AMAZING ORIGAMI FOR CHILDREN
Steve and Megumi Biddle

Origami is an exciting and easy way to make toys, decorations and all kinds of useful things from folded paper.

Use leftover gift paper to make a party hat and a fancy box. Or create a colourful lorry, a pretty rose and a zoo full of origami animals. There are over 50 fun projects in Amazing Origami.

Following Steve and Megumi's step-by-step instructions and clear drawings, you'll amaze your friends and family with your magical paper creations.

ISBN 0 09 966180 2   £5.99

MAGICAL STRING   Steve and Megumi Biddle

With only a loop of string you can make all kinds of shapes, puzzles and games. Steve and Megumi Biddle provide all the instructions and diagrams that are needed to create their amazing string magic in another of their inventive and absorbing books.

ISBN 0 09 964470 3   £2.50